CHARLIE
the CH🍪MP'I🍪N

When winning comes with a consequence

By: Julia E. Giancaspro
Illustrated by: stefanie st. denis

A special thank you for the writing assistance provided by Karen Stephenson of The Happy Guy Marketing Inc.

Tellwell Talent
www.tellwell.ca

ISBN
978-0-2288-7148-4 (Hardcover)
978-0-2288-5150-9 (Paperback)

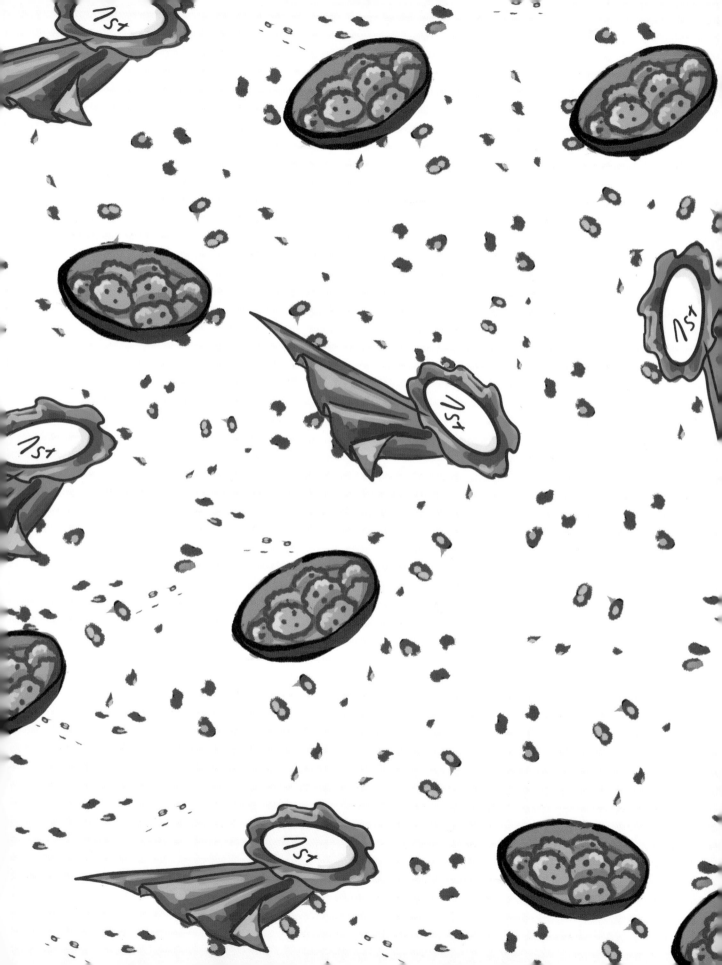

Charlie, Chukums and Cali are not only best friends, but they are also sisters. Charlie and Chukums are Chihuahuas and Cali is an American bobtail cat.

They share a lot of things, such as toys, getting groomed, and having so much fun in the backyard.

One thing they don't share is their food bowl.

Cali never has to worry about protecting her food as the Chihuahuas are not interested in cat food.

However, Chukums sometimes finds it difficult to save some food for later because Charlie always eats whatever is left in the dog bowls. Some days, Charlie even tries to nudge Chukums out of Chukums' bowl. Even if only a morsel of food remains, Charlie will lick those bowls clean.

Without a doubt, Charlie loves food. She always looks forward to mealtime and she'll even sulk and bark for her food every day. Whenever she hears a bag or the fridge open, she flies into the kitchen at top speed; and at the dinner table, she holds up her paw and begs as though she hasn't eaten for days.

One afternoon, in the backyard, Charlie, Chukums and their good friends and neighbours Ruby and Sisi gathered at the fence.

Ruby, a pug and Boston terrier mix, lived next door with her sister, Sisi, a schnauzer. Ruby shared some great news that made Charlie so excited. Ruby had heard from Jax, a cockapoo friend, that there was going to be a cookie-eating contest the next day at Bark Park.

Chukums sighed and shook her head. "Charlie could be making a very poor choice entering that contest," she thought and trotted off to tell Mom and Dad about this.

Charlie found out that not only were Ruby and Sisi entering this contest but so were Jax and Baloo, an English bull mastiff.

Charlie turned toward the house begging Mom and Dad, "Please, please, please! I just know I can win!"

Mom looked at Dad then down toward Charlie. "I don't think this is a good idea, Charlie. You already have some extra weight and cookies are not a healthy treat, especially if you're eating as many as you can."

Chukums and Cali were snickering in the kitchen, peeping from inside the house. They loved Charlie, but they knew this cookie-eating contest was not a good idea. They did like the thought of winning a one-year supply of treats though.

Well," Dad started, "I know you are confident you can win, but after this, you'll not get any treats for a whole week."

Charlie barked for joy!

The next day, Charlie, Chukums, Mom and Dad met up with Ruby, Sisi, Jax and Baloo at Bark Park. Charlie was boasting that she was going to win. Baloo glanced down at Charlie and thought she was bonkers. He thought he would win because he was much bigger than her.

All the dogs took their spot at a very long table. With the wagging tails and Charlie's drool dripping on the wooden table, it was quite the scene. All the moms and dads stood behind to hold the contestants so that as the judge passed out the cookies no one would start before the whistle blew.

When the whistle did blow, Chukums was amazed at how fast Charlie's mouth began chomping away. After a couple of minutes, Chukums was getting worried that Charlie might be overdoing it. After three minutes, the whistle blew to signal the end of the contest.

The judge smiled as he walked up and down counting how many cookies were left in each bowl.

He stopped at Baloo's spot and was impressed to see only three cookies left. Without taking another step, right beside Baloo the judge noticed an empty bowl.

"The winner!" he exclaimed as he handed Charlie the first-place ribbon.

Everyone cheered and even Chukums was happy that her sister had won. Charlie didn't look very happy though.

Oh no," Mom said, holding Charlie in her arms, feeling rather alarmed. "I knew it. We shouldn't have allowed Charlie to enter this contest."

Everyone nervously gathered around.

Charlie had a stomach ache that hurt so much she was not able to move. Mom had to carry her home and put her straight to bed.

Dad and Chukums followed shortly after as they had to get the prize to bring home. When they walked in the door with the big bag of treats, Charlie couldn't even lift her head.

Cali was shocked to see her sister not get excited about food coming in the front door.

Charlie learned a valuable lesson that day. She vowed to never eat that fast ever again, to never sneak food out of Chukums' bowl again, and to never beg for food again. Charlie learned that eating too much junk food was not a smart thing to do, even if it was a contest.

It took two weeks before Charlie even glanced at all the treats she had won.

The End

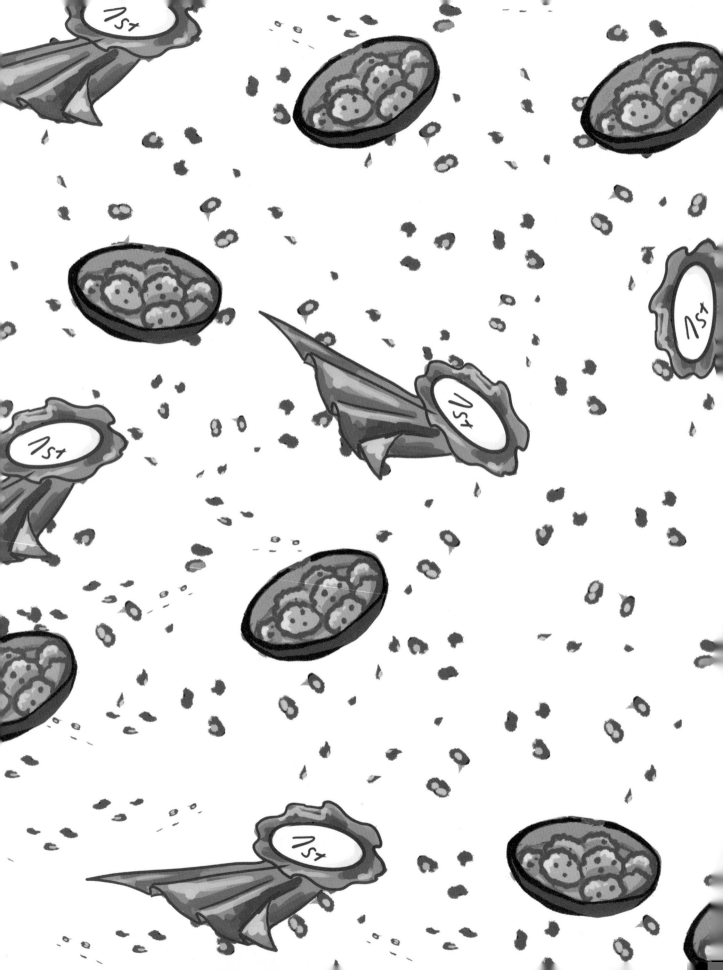

In memory of a furry friend:

Dogs and cats are my favourite animals. I was inspired to write a children's book depicting the life of my own pets. Most people reading my book can relate to the love they share with their furry friends. Our pets often bring so much happiness and a sense of wholeness to our hearts and we only want the best for them. They are part of our family. Charlie was one of my two beloved long-haired Chihuahuas. This particular book inspired me to write about my beloved long-haired Chihuahua dog named Charlie. She was a very good dog with a sweet, kind, loving and funny personality. She was a special friend and companion and loved her family unconditionally. Although this story is fictional, we cannot hide the truth that Charlie never missed a bite. We will never forget her, and we will always smile at the memory of her enthusiasm for food.

Follow us!
Instagram @chukumscharliecali